ALL THINGS

WEIRD &

STRANGE

All Things Weird & Strange

Jessica Marie Baumgartner, Shelly X Leonn, Michael Hilton, Amanda Lance, Stephanie Hansen, & LL Montez

ISBN 978-1-7350423-4-3 (print)

ISBN 978-1-3934311-3-8 (eBook)

Printed in the U.S.A.
First printing, 2021

The text type was set in Perpetua and Times New Roman.

Cover design by Hypothesis Cover Designs

For the dreamers.

Never let the doubters hold you back.

∞   ∞

SWAP by Michael Hilton

Mattie stared at her phone in complete shock. She couldn't believe Ari Rae—*the* Ari Rae—was on Swap. Two million followers on every social app, and the teen idol had finally created a Swap account. A check mark was next to her name so it was definitely real. Mattie sat on her bed, her thumb trembling, hovering over the screen, over the button that would request a Swap. She took a deep breath, tapped it, and giggled for the first time in…well, it felt like months since she'd laughed or smiled. If Ari Rae—*the* Ari Rae—selected her to *Swap* Memrys, Mattie's life would turn around instantly, she just knew it.

Sure, the contest was probably a publicity stunt. The queen of viral dance holograms announcing she would open one lucky follower's Memry? And then send

1

that same lucky follower an exclusive Memry nobody else could open? That just had to be an easy way to get a ton of followers fast. She'd probably end up picking someone she knew. It wasn't like *the* Ari Rae would stream a Memry from just any rando, right? Besides, Mattie was pretty sure she'd read one of Ari Rae's interviews saying that streaming someone else's memory across a consciousness-transfer app was bad for your aura…or something. But whatever. Even just thirty seconds to live as Ari Rae would propel Mattie from the bottom of the sophomore class food chain to the heights of popularity.

Mattie returned her attention to her phone and wrinkled her nose at the window asking her to submit a photo of herself for the contest. *Ugh.* She tapped the Add Photo icon and scrolled through her album, finding something wrong with every picture of herself.

Face too red.
Nose too big.

Double chin. Gross.
Ew, why did I wear that swimsuit?

Excitement evaporated with every disappointing picture. Who was she kidding? Ari Rae was *gorgeous*. Every boy in school followed her Hologram account. Mattie was just meh. No, worse than meh. She was an *uggo*. She knew what the girls called her behind her back. *Frootie-Os*. Brandi McCalister, the queen bee herself, had coined the term, a kinda-sorta-clever jab at Mattie's parrot nose. Or toucan. Or whatever the bird on the cereal box was. It was enough to bring stinging tears to her eyes.

Why would Ari Rae ever choose to *Swap* with her? The girl already had half a million followers in the four hours since she'd created a Swap account. Her odds were next to nothing.

Mattie sighed, picked the least ugly photo—*still ugly*—and was about to toss her phone away when the next screen prompted for a Memry to upload.

She groaned. This time, she did toss her phone, falling back on her mattress as the phone landed with a *thunk* on the floor. How was she supposed to pick a memory good enough for *the* Ari Rae? Her life was total glam. Mattie's life was…school, homework, and rewatching holo versions of The Office a million times. Thirty seconds of Ari Rae's world would probably be photo shoots and dance choreographies. Did Mattie even have thirty seconds of anything interesting in her life?

Oh, she could upload when she brushed Devin Johnson's elbow on the way to Biology last week. Briefly touching the hottest guy in school? Yeah. Real interesting. Ari Rae probably brushed elbows with more hot guys than Mattie would ever see in her whole life. Besides, the parental controls her mom set up would probably block Swap from transmitting any sensation data anyway. Ari Rae wouldn't even get the complete experience of being Southwood

High's sophomore parrot. Or toucan. Whatever.

You know what? Screw it. She'd upload her worst Memry from the past week, the one where Brandi pointed out the giant red zit on her nose in front of the whole class by asking if she wanted some cortisone cream. That horrible girl had an obsession with drawing attention to Mattie's bird nose.

Maybe Ari Rae would appreciate knowing what it was like to want to die.

Mattie scooted off the bed, picked up her phone, and tapped the screen. Reaching behind her ear to the implanted Memry drive—hers was *so* old, when would her parents get her a new one?—she synced the device with Swap's embedded Memry feature. The window loaded a thirty-second clip of the incident, asking if she wanted to trim the selection. Mattie winced at the laughing faces of her class. No, she wouldn't trim anything. Let Ari Rae feel humiliation for once.

Mattie swiped the Memry up, submitting it to the contest.

She leaned against her bedframe, hugging her knees to her chest as she absently scrolled through Swap. Brandi's Memrys dominated her feed. Why did she even follow her? Oh, right, Devin. Southwood's star quarterback appeared in a Memry, sitting across from Brandi at some burger place. The video-only feature showed him looking straight into the "camera"—Mattie hated thinking he was looking into Brandi's gorgeous blue eyes—and flashed that brilliant smile. Brandi had probably said something stupid. Boys liked it when a girl acted stupid.

Mattie's heart ached. She so wanted this Memry to be hers. Her thumb hesitated over the *Stream Memry* icon. In an instant, she could have Brandi's memory streamed into her mind. She could be right there in that burger joint having Devin smile at her.

She wrenched her thumb away. She wouldn't give Brandi the satisfaction that Frootie-Os had streamed her Memry.

Instead, she toggled the holo feature. Her phone's projectors whirred, and a miniature holographic preview of the Memry bloomed above the screen. Devin's dark flawless skin, his heartbreakingly beautiful jawline, and that perfect smile filled the space before her. She could lean forward, just centimeters, and their lips would… No. No way. The holo feature might not track that she watched the Memry, but there was no way, *no way*, she could live with herself if Brandi somehow found out Mattie was kissing a holographic version of her boyfriend.

Her phone buzzed, and Mattie let out a surprised yelp, the phone tumbling from her hands.

A notification appeared through Devin's transparent holographic face. Mattie bent over the phone, swiped the Memry away, and stared at the text.

Ari Rae has added you as a friend.

The room spun, and Mattie's vision went blurry. A scream worked its way up to her throat and came out in full force as she bounced on the floor.

"Ohmygoshohmygoshohmygosh."

"Mattie?" a muffled voice called over hurried footsteps outside. Her mom burst through the door. "Are you okay?"

With a furious grin, Mattie held up her phone. "Ari Rae added me on Swap!"

Her mom's concerned expression slipped to confusion then gave way to an eye roll. "You remember what I said about no boys on that thing? Sharon's mom said they post memories of going to the bathroom just to freak out—"

"*Mem-rees*," Mattie corrected with the proper pronunciation. "Mom, this is huge. She may DM me any minute. Go." She shooed at her mom.

"Don't wave me away, Mattie," her mom snapped.

"Okay, I'm sorry, but please," Mattie pleaded, "I need to be alone right now."

Her mom jabbed a finger at her phone. "No boys on that thing," she said before leaving.

Mattie hurried to close the door, then flopped onto her bed, staring at the new *Friends* status on Ari Rae's profile. She didn't think her smile could get bigger until a notification popped up in her DMs.

She let out a squeal and opened her messages. There it was. A DM from *the* Ari Rae.

Wanna swap? it read, followed by *Accept* and *Ignore*.

"I won the contest," Mattie whispered, not quite believing the words. By this evening, she'd probably be in articles in all the newsfeeds. Everyone would know she *Swapped* with a celebrity. Devin would know…

Wait. How did this happen? Why would Ari Rae choose her to swap Memrys with? She double-checked the profile, but the verified check mark stared back at her, confirming that this was real. Maybe the universe was finally giving her a break.

She tapped *Accept* and giggled as Ari Rae's Memry loaded. Her life was about to change forever. She was about to live as Ari Rae for thirty seconds in an exclusive Memry. There was no way she wouldn't be the talk of Southwood. Brandi would be so jealous. And Devin would definitely talk to Mattie now. She could see the look on Brandi's face as Devin flashed Mattie that smile instead of—

She was staring down at her feet. Only, they weren't her feet. They were Ari Rae's in designer flats. Mattie gaped at her—well, Ari Rae's—long, smooth, flawless legs. She was streaming *the* Ari Rae's Memry.

A thrill ran through her, but Ari Rae's emotions quickly drowned out the echo of excitement from Mattie's own body. *Wow*, Mattie thought. Most people switched the emotion feature off when they posted Memrys unless they were really, really good emotions. Or really sad. She'd heard of people getting addicted to streaming Memrys for the emotional highs and lows. But this? Mattie couldn't quite put her finger on it, but the feeling was like acid in the pit of her stomach. Whatever Ari Rae was feeling in this moment was way more complex than the simple happy and sad emotions Swap could usually stream. Maybe there had been an update?

Whatever. Her own thrill returned when Ari Rae looked up at the body-length mirror. She wore an adorable black crop top and the cutest high-waisted jean shorts Mattie had ever seen. Ari Rae was gorgeous. Mattie *felt* gorgeous being her, the way the clothes hugged her perfect curves, the way her lips shaped in a bow, the way her nose felt proportional to her face, curving up just a little into a perfect tip. She was glowed up more than Mattie could ever hope to be. So why did Ari Rae's features look so sad?

Ari Rae's eyes turned from the mirror and, through them, Mattie glimpsed a set washed in lights and surrounded by cameras.

Yes! A photo shoot!

But again excitement from Mattie's body died with that overwhelming sensation streaming from Ari Rae's memory. Her head felt foggy, her muscles ached, and something gnawed at her core. Mattie thought there was a glitch in the stream, some kind of sensation data that wasn't coming through properly, until Ari Rae glanced over at the catering table, a telltale longing pulling her toward its sandwiches and fruit and pastries.

A feeling popped unbidden deep into Mattie's core, a sense she couldn't quite articulate but that felt familiar. It reminded her of the time Brandi had called attention to her love handles in the new outfit Mattie had bought for PE. The rest of the week,

Mattie had refused to eat, pretending she wasn't hungry at lunch or the dinner table.

One bite, a thought surfaced in Mattie's head. Only, it wasn't hers. It was Ari Rae's. Weird. She didn't think a user's *thoughts* were streamable. Must be a new feature.

Oh gosh, is Ari Rae hearing my thoughts in the Memry I gave her? This time it was Mattie's voice that bounced in her panicked mind, but she didn't have time to dwell on figuring out how this was possible because another of Ari Rae's thoughts crashed into her brain.

One bite, and I could pur—

"Ari Rae, you ready?" the photographer called from the set, interrupting the thought.

Suddenly, Mattie put it together, recognized the sensation gnawing at her—Ari Rae's—stomach. She was hungry. And she'd been hungry for a long, long time.

Ari Rae turned toward the set, and Mattie felt the idol's eyes painfully tear away from the catering table. She felt the burning muscles dragging her flawless body over to the cameras.

Ari Rae doesn't drag herself. She bounces into frame.

Before Mattie could wonder at this further, an emotion swirled in Ari Rae's chest, solidifying into something heavy that crushed her heart. Was it...*despair*?

The emotion intensified as a boy came onto the set. Mattie's own heart did a flip at the sight of Zack Yun. Was Ari Rae actually doing a photo shoot with the most famous K-Pop star in the world? His hit single *Ignite Me* was on the charts for months. Mattie's emotions quickly faded into the background when she felt Ari Rae manage a weak smile at the singer.

Zack Yun didn't even try to hide his eye roll. He said something in Korean to an assistant standing just off set, and the way his lips pulled into a cynical smirk made Mattie think that this photo shoot was a joke to him. She felt a sinking feeling coming from Ari Rae, and it took her a moment to identify it. Did Ari Rae feel like a fraud?

The photographer said something, and Mattie felt Ari Rae straighten. No more dragging around. She'd transformed into the bouncy bubble of energy she was known for in all her videos. But as she posed with Zack, their manufactured chemistry creating stunning shots on the review monitor, she felt all her limbs ache. She felt the bit of Ari Rae's brain constantly noting the catering table, tracking the crew members' lattes, wondering if she could afford the calories for a single bite of the protein bar in her purse.

Ari Rae's thoughts twisted through Mattie's head, spikes of failure, loneliness, depression, clawing hunger…how did she live with them all? She had two million followers on almost every social media account. She made almost two thousand dollars every time she posted. How could she…want to die?

Mattie flashed back to Brandi pointing out her zit, to her class laughing, to her own feeling of wanting life to end. Her breath came quick, though it felt distant from all of Ari Rae's painful sensations. She had to get out of this Memry, had to block the emotion feature, somehow stop the idol's dark thoughts from drowning her.

She was about to scream, but the next instant, she was back on her bed. She bolted upright and looked around her room, Ari Rae's pain and despair and hunger fading like a bad dream. A glance down at her phone told her the Memry had ended. How long had it lasted? Those thirty seconds had seemed like forever. It took her a moment to realize a message from Ari Rae was waiting for her.

I watched your Memry. You should post it, let everyone know what it's like. Let's learn to love ourselves, ok?

Tears welled in Mattie's eyes, trickling down as she stared at the message. Finally, she swiped it away and scrolled through her feed. A *Thoughts* beta icon was now appearing in the corner of new posts. She stopped on Brandi's, uploaded four minutes ago, a Memry of her by the pool, bronzed legs dipping into the water. Despite everything, a faint twinge of jealousy pricked at Mattie, but the lingering sensations of Ari Rae's Memry quenched it. She'd always assumed Brandi's life was perfect. Captain of the drill team, dating Devin Johnson, perfect hair, smooth skin. But now, she realized she didn't know anything about Brandi beyond what she saw. Part of her wanted to stream the Memry, hear what Brandi was thinking. Maybe she really did have a perfect life. Maybe the things she was posting weren't just curated from her best moments. Maybe if Mattie streamed her Memrys, all Brandi's thoughts really would be full of sunshine and rainbows and happiness. Then again, she'd thought the same thing about Ari Rae.

She eyed the Memry she'd sent Ari Rae, the preview playing a loop of laughing classmates. She could make it public, *Thoughts* and all. What would Brandi think? She hated that she even cared.

She read Ari Rae's message again.

Let's learn to love ourselves, ok?

Mattie selected the Memry she'd uploaded, watched Brandi point at her nose, saw the laughing faces in the class. With a resolute breath, she tapped *Make Public*.

Well, it was out there now. Maybe she'd given Brandi more ammunition to make fun of her. But maybe her post would reach others, would pass on what Ari Rae had shown her. She stared at the caption she'd written. *Life isn't all Frootie-Os.*

A heart floated up from the post, and Mattie smiled at the like from *the* Ari Rae.

MICHAEL HILTON'S BIO

Michael Hilton is a time traveler from the future who has come back to warn us of the impending literary apocalypse. A huge nerd for Young Adult Science Fiction and Fantasy, he writes to stave off the coming wasteland of soulless fiction. One day his Wikipedia page will describe his warnings as "mildly prophetic," and "wildly exaggerated." He is the author of the Bobby Robot series and publisher of The Weekly Geek. Michael lives on earth but is thinking about moving soon.

https://www.michaelhiltonbooks.com/

VOCAL ROOTS by Jessica Marie

Baumgartner

"You need to go to a doctor," her manager, Cleon, said the second she appeared from her final encore.

Zaria, still high from a universe of applause, scoffed at him. "Have you had your little problem looked at yet?" She gestured to his groin.

The shadows on his face disappeared as he stepped forward and gently grasped her shoulders. "I look after you first, my dear. That was my promise."

Zaria laughed, but her voice pinched like a flattened straw. Another coughing fit overcame her. She hacked and wheezed, gasping for air like an old lady with pneumonia.

Cleon patted her back and grabbed the hot teacup from her dressing room table. "That's what you get for mocking the vow I made to your brother. He adored you. What would he say now?"

"To go to a doctor," Zaria said in a husky voice. "But he always worried too much. I'm not a little girl anymore."

Cleon watched her sip her tea. "Just because this industry loves youth doesn't mean you're grown. You caught a few breaks thanks to your talent and *our* oversight, but you're not even eighteen yet." His features relaxed. "I loved your brother, but I love you *too*. Now stop being so damn stubborn. You're jeopardizing your career...and mine." A knock sounded and Cleon glared at the door.

Zaria cleared her throat. She pulled at the curls surrounding her face and smiled like nothing was wrong. "Come in."

Cleon gaped at her.

"Oh darling, you were perfect!"

Zaria nodded at her producer, Lynn, and kissed her on the cheek.

"You're ready for dinner, right? We must celebrate while I'm in town, but I promise I won't keep you out too late. You have to keep that voice fresh for tomorrow." Lynn flit about her dressed in silks and jewelry that made her resemble a bedazzled toad.

Zaria smiled. "Of course."

Cleon slid behind Lynn pretending to shoot her in the back of the head with his hands.

Zaria closed her eyes and inhaled.

Lynn grabbed her hand and pulled her toward the door. She stopped and stared at Cleon like he hadn't been there the whole time. "Oh, it's you." She turned to Zaria. "I thought you'd have fired him by now."

Zaria shook her head. "Of course not."

Cleon barred the door.

"You'd make a lovely bouncer at the club we're going to." Lynn reached around him and ducked under his arm.

22

He leaned close to Zaria and whispered, "She is killing you and your voice."

Zaria glanced around her dressing room. The makeup jars sat sprawled about. Her robe was wrinkled on the floor. She longed for a quiet bath, but singing alone in the tub seemed so pedestrian now.

"Please don't go," Cleon said as Lynn tugged at Zaria's hand.

Only the untended bonsai tree in the corner of the room didn't try to control Zaria. She blinked, trapped in the moment. Her throat pulsed, rubbed raw, and her left ear was building pressure. She gaped at the tree and her head rang.

The plant glowed with a brilliant emerald sheen. The roots screamed from the potting soil.

Zaria tensed and turned away. *Now I know I need to see a doctor*. She shimmied past Cleon and blew him a kiss. "Don't worry. I'll get a checkup tomorrow."

He grabbed the vase of flowers by the door and smashed them behind her.

Lynn laughed. "Someone's being a bit dramatic."

"He's just worried about me." Zaria quickened her pace.

***

"It's not just a symptom. This is my livelihood!" Zaria glared at Dr. Preffit.

"It could be temporary. With viruses like this, people experience a wide range of symptoms. I'm prescribing you a mild steroid, an anti-inflammatory for the swelling, and vocal rest."

Zaria rubbed her throat and gasped. "I don't have time for vocal rest. I don't have time for this."

You do now, she could hear her brother's voice as if they were back in the studio together. She scanned the room and cocked her head at the peace lily sitting beside the computer on the exam room desk.

Dr. Preffit went on and on about following orders to keep her voice healthy, but with one ear completely clogged, Zaria's concentration fell on the plant. Its stem

24

glowed. The dirt hissed. She wondered if she should ask for a recommendation for a psychiatrist instead. *The vocal rest is impossible enough,* she told herself.

Dr. Preffit's speech neared its end, "We're all rooting for you, Zaria. Please take some time to heal and you'll be belting higher than ever."

Zaria nodded. "Thank you. I appreciate it. I'm sorry about the—"

"No need to apologize." Dr. Preffit handed her the scripts. "It's scary. But that's why I'm here to help." She opened the door and led her back to the waiting room.

Cleon stood, hat wrinkled in his hands. Zaria held her head high and walked toward him as if she were onstage.

"Well?" He raised his eyebrows.

She crumpled the prescriptions in her hand and hid them in her pocket. "I need a few meds, but I'm not missing my show tonight."

"That's it?" He followed her out the door.

"Yeah." She giggled, then stifled a cough. "Just a little fatigue."

"Fatigue?" His steps pounded on the ground. "Why does it feel like you're leaving something out?"

"Because you're worried. You always worry. It's your *job* to worry."

A car was waiting for them at the curb, but a couple of people already stood ready, cameras in hand. They shot picture after picture before Zaria could conceal herself in the vehicle. Cleon got in behind her and shut the door, staring back and forth.

"Are you a manager or a body-guard?" She laughed, but the pressure pierced her ear. She leaned her head against the headrest and sighed. Each bump, every jostle felt like a knife in the ear.

"What kind of pills they give you?" He held out his hand.

Zaria fingered her pocket making sure to keep the prescriptions hidden. "Oh nothing. Just some vocal rest. *After* tonight." She didn't like keeping things from Cleon but the thought of taking a steroid before going onstage grew too frustrating. She imagined him following her around like a concerned stage mother as Lynn scolded her for not fitting into her dress.

"That's it?" Cleon eyed her with an eyebrow raised.

Her cell phone lit up and she was glad for the interruption. She held it up and shrugged. Lynn was already texting about the show. Zaria messaged back that everything was on schedule.

Warm ups at noon: Lynn reminded her, as if she could forget.

Zaria closed her eyes and hummed to herself. She had to fight to not grab her ear at the pain, but music was her life. *I'll be fine. I'm a professional*, she told herself. *A legend. And legends improvise.*

Cleon's gaze weighed on her for the rest of the ride. For the entire trip to the stadium, his watchful eyes remained fixed on her. They were dropped off at the back entrance but she felt as if she were under a microscope.

Just before stepping into the venue she stopped. "Are you sure you're ready for this?"

Cleon put his hands on his hips.

She glanced between him and the door. "Maybe it's too much for *you* and that's why you're so worried."

"It's my job to worry." He winked. He opened the door for her, and Lynn stepped through. He cringed.

She brushed past to embrace Zaria. "Tonight will be unforgettable."

Cleon remained holding the door, but his features tightened. "Let's stay on schedule then."

Lynn turned to him. "Oh, hi." She opened her clutch purse and tipped him.

His face reddened with ire. Zaria grabbed the money from his hand and thanked Lynn. "I guess drinks are on you tonight." She followed her to sound check with Cleon grumbling behind.

Zaria let a few notes fly before reaching her stool. Her pianist picked up right with her and they practiced scales up and down her low and high registers, but she struggled to match notes. She pressed on her ear and breathed deep to compensate.

Lynn watched her with a smirk. The rest of the band started. Cleon cocked his head, but Zaria refused to give in.

She went higher and higher building the notes with a crescendo mingled in glissandos. She hit the highest aspect of her range and pushed as hard as she could. Something popped. A great blast burst through both ears, her head pounded, and she blacked out.

***

Zaria shut herself away. After her eardrums burst, life held no meaning. No more songs. No more sweet notes. No more late-night belting. She had pushed herself too far. Her hearing was shot.

Lynn and the record label released Zaria from her contract before she could recover. Her fans forgot her the second a hot new singer was introduced. Even Cleon distanced himself. He was expressly animated about his anger over her withholding the vocal rest order, which broke in the tabloids thanks to a mouthy nurse.

Zaria stood in her bathroom staring at the medicine cabinet. *I could end it so easily*. Her heart yearned to be buried with her brother. She glanced over her shoulder. Her four-post bed and Victorian furniture laughed at her.

Everything was a lie, but the nightstand glowed with a strange light. She turned. Her eyes warmed under its luminescence. The tiny bamboo plant sat alone in a ceramic pot.

The plant that had been sent to her dressing room from an adoring fan now kept her spirits alive. The blaze deepened.

It sprawled throughout the room, reaching for her. Echoes of words indecipherable sang at the base of her brain.

It's impossible, she thought. *My hearing is gone…even if I regain some function, I've lost my record deal and everyone who believed in me.*

She laughed bitterly at the idea of hearing. It all had to be written now, written or typed. Who had time for that? Who had time to learn sign language or remember a broken singer?

The light consumed her before she fully gave in to self-pity. It made her skin bright. Her head swam and she smiled. Her feet seemed to move on their own. Each step rooted her in a new life. A strange comfort surged through her limbs until she reached the plant.

It sat before her, tempting and unknown. Like Sleeping Beauty with the spindle, Zaria knew she had to touch it, but deep inside she also realized that life would never regain its old charm.

The bamboo called.

She answered, pulling it completely from the dish. She ogled the tiny white roots exposed before the world. The air grew thick. Her body went heavy, but something in her mind said, "Touch them."

She gripped the stalk tight and raised her other hand. It shook before the tiny network. Her index finger reached the nearest root and a burst of energy shot through her. A hundred voices erupted through her brain.

She pulled back. *What was that?*

She closed her eyes and touched all five fingers to the roots. Her body sang with voices, words, language; music. She fell to the ground and cradled the plant, listening to its many thoughts. For hours she remained still, just happy to listen.

After a while she could better decipher what to follow. By the next morning, the plant *spoke* to her. Its godly voice harmonized within her body. It echoed through her brain. "Sing with us."

I can't. She coughed back tears and clutched at her ears.

The second she let go of the plant her body went cold. The world lost its color.

She reached for the bamboo and stared in awe. *Maybe I already killed myself. But what the hell kind of afterlife is this?*

She tickled the roots. Her body was thrust back into the pulse of euphoria. "Sing with us," Zaria felt the words more than heard them.

It occurred to her that her voice remained. Her words would never leave. Without anything to lose, she breathed deep. Her diaphragm expanded. She sat up tall, leveled her chin, and pushed out the notes. She practiced again and again but changed the words to thank the plant.

Its light shined brighter and brighter. Visions of underground realms full of roots waiting for connection shocked Zaria. Her audience had forgotten her, but the trees never would; the bamboo told her so. They remembered everything, everyone.

She made up her mind. She would sell her apartment in New York and find a cottage in the country. Fully furnished with modern electric, plumbing, and Wi-Fi (she refused to give up modern conveniences). She knew her true calling.

***

Ten years after her tragic illness she was unrecognizable. The tabloids ran a piece asking: Where is Zaria now? But she could not be found in any cities, clubs, or hot spots. If they knew how "low" their diva had sunk, they would never have understood.

Zaria brushed her hair out. She pulled it tight behind her head and put on a hard hat. She tightened her boots and adjusted her overalls. *Ready for another legendary performance*, she told herself as she approached the cellar.

She opened the stone door and walked past jars and cans of preserves, through the back opening, into a dirt tunnel. It narrowed. She got on her hands and knees and crawled along, following the burrow through rock and root until the dark path opened to a small den secured with numerous roots running along the floor, walls, and ceiling.

Great thick trees stretched down into the earth, awaiting her, along with small snaky vines growing from bushes and flowers. Even some mushrooms and a colony of lichen grew to hear the vibrations of her exotic songs. She clicked on the flashlight at her side, propped it against a stone for a spotlight, and readied herself to do what she was born to do for the beings who adored her no matter what she wore, who she hung out with, or how she practiced.

Her gratitude would be heard in the muffled tones of her changed voice. She loved them for just wanting to share her passion. She was grateful for finding a deeper meaning.

JESSICA MARIE BAUMGARTNER'S BIO

Jessica's motto is: Adventure first, then write! When not running around exploring nature, she chases multiple versions of herself and feeds animal babies. She is also the author of Walk Your Path, The Golden Rule, The Embracing Entropy Series, My Family Is Different and more. She works as a columnist for LitReactor Magazine & Witch Way Magazine, and is a current member of the Missouri Writer's Guild & the SCBWI.

She loves writing all kinds of stories but focuses mainly on adult non-fiction and children's. As a dyslexic Pagan, Jess loves all types of people, but also writes about spiritual issues and the fun of a brain that works differently.

https://jessicamariebaumgartner.com/

IT'S A TWIN THING by Shelly X

Leonn

The stout woman reaches across the chipped coffee table separating us. I clasp her hand. Her grip is warm, and the folds in her palms are soft.

"It's wonderful to meet you, Revez." As her arm pumps, her cardigan flaps, releasing a wave of warmth. She smells like an attic—quiet, insular, and stuffed with memories.

"You, as well, Dr. Patke." A genuine smile stretches across my face. Few people see my full smile.

"Have a seat, young lady." She gestures to a worn, tan armchair covered in what appears to be a hand-stitched afghan.

I fall into it, and the cushion melds around my body.

After taking a seat in an oversized rocker, Dr. Patke regards me, her watery, hazel eyes roaming over my lanky, lean frame, stringy dishwater hair, and pale skin. I take in her presence of fluffy gray curls, colorful scarves, and blue hush puppy shoes. Nothing about this shared moment of study seems unnatural or awkward. Instead, we seem to adjust to each other's presence, becoming more comfortable in our shared space.

"Tell me what brings you here." She holds no notebook, but her perceptive gaze takes me in with precision beyond that which is possible with a pen and paper.

I lean forward, bending my long frame at the hips, and wrap my spindly fingers around my crossed knees. "I can't sleep."

She chuckles, which causes her pliable throat to jiggle. "I think that's implied, don't you?"

I glance around, taking in the multiple doctoral degrees, the bookshelf brimming with neuroscience texts, and the framed reproduction of Salvador Dali's work "Sleep." "Definitely implied. I didn't even know there was such a thing as a sleep lab."

"*Lab* sounds so clinical." She tilts her head to the side, and her empathetic smirk crinkles the corners of her mouth. "Mad scientists in white coats and all that."

"Something like that." I shrug, then search the room again. This time, I seek out an entrance into the rest of the facility. The term "sleep lab" makes me think of tomb-shaped monitoring chambers with patients stuffed inside, electrodes pasted to their temples.

"You can stop trying to find the trapdoor, dear," Dr. Patke says. "This is it."

I open my mouth to ask her how she knew my question without me asking it, but I close it, remembering I've never been subtle with my emotions.

She continues, "It's just you, me, and the wonderful expanse of the subconscious world."

"There's nothing wonderful about it to me," I mutter as I fold my arms across my midsection.

Dr. Patke shows no reaction to my assertion. "Why not?"

Because I've already decided to trust Dr. Patke, I allow my story to pour out of me. "Every night, I take hours and hours to go to sleep. And when I finally do, it's awful." I squeeze my eyes shut, as unbidden images from the dark dreamscapes flash through my memory. "It's the same rotating nightmares. The setting is always a beach, a party, or a mansion."

"Those sound relatively pleasant." Dr. Patke raises a skeptical eyebrow, but I can hear a coating of mirth on her tone.

"There's nothing pleasant about these places." I shake my head. "Each one is horrible. Also, while I'm sleeping, I'm kicking around and thrashing, like I'm trying to fight." I tug up my yoga pants leg, exposing a rainbow of streaks and bruises running up my calf, shin, knee, and thigh.

"The other leg is just as bad. And my brother—"

"Dormir?" Dr. Patke prompts. "Your twin?"

"Right. It's the same for him. But he doesn't hurt himself. Instead, he sleep-walks. One night he fell down the stairs at home and broke his elbow."

"Which is what prompted Sheila to call me." Dr. Patke turns her palms upward as if to say the weight of our troubles has fallen into her capable grasp. "The future for you, your brother, your stepmother, and the world begins today, Revez."

I realize that I am to release all of my burdens into her waiting hands. Yet, a question nags at me. "How is it possible for you to do your—" I pause, searching for the right phrasing, "—work or therapy with just this?" I gesture around the office, which seems to be completely lacking in any type of electronic gadget, not even a wall phone.

Her smile radiates patience. "The work we are about to begin takes place in the realm of the subconscious. Our minds are all we need. I will be your guide, the Virgil to your Dante, as you conquer your fears."

I catch the reference to Dante's masterpiece *The Inferno*. Instead of disturbing me, the nod strikes me as aligned to my plight. Sleep has become my hell. Maybe Dr. Patke can lead me through it as well as out the other side. "What happens first?" I ask, eagerness tightening my throat.

"It's quite simple." Dr. Patke lets her hands drop onto her knees, and she leans forward on her chair's rockers, causing them to creak softly. "I will lead you through each of your dream worlds. We will conquer the obstacles holding you back within each one and transform your nightmares into experiences of expression."

"Expression of what?" I ask, eyes wide.

42

"Of power, dear." She ruffles her scarf to accentuate her point. "What else?"

"What kind of power?"

"The greatest power of them all." She taps on her forehead, in the spot mystics claim to be the location of the third eye. "But enough questions. We haven't a moment to lose." Brushing the lint from her orange pull-on corduroys, she stands, causing the rocker to pitch back and forth. One of her hands with its dimples for knuckles extends toward me. "Are you ready?"

I furrow my brow. "What do you mean?"

The watery shine to her eyes glints when her gaze locks onto mine. "Decide if you're ready, Revez. Then, clasp my hand."

Determination makes my heart swell. "I'm ready." Her grip—strong, not soft like during our initial handshake—holds me fast and focused.

My consciousness fades. At the lingering corners of it, I hear voices.

"Is she ready, Dr. Patke?"

That voice, I know it. That's Sheila, my stepmother. How is that possible?

"Yes, she has accepted our subconscious manipulations. She no longer recognizes me, and she has recast you as an evil stepmother figure. This office is her complete reality now, and she is eager to follow me through the exercises we have planned."

Is that Dr. Patke? Why is Dr. Patke talking to Sheila?

"What about her brother?"

"Engaged in REM and ready to make the connection into his sister's subconscious world."

"It will be tricky keeping him from interfering, while also opening his abilities."

"Tricky, but not impossible. I am confident we will unlock their powers before the night is through."

None of this makes sense. Suddenly, I come to the only logical conclusion. *Of course, this entire conversation is all part of my dreams. I'm sure the real journey will begin soon, just like Dr. Patke promised.*

"Then, let's begin."

The voices go silent.

A ray of condensed heat pierces the top of my spine. The heat sears and tears. I open my mouth to cry out.

The sensation ceases.

I find myself standing on an aged, wooden deck. The scent of saltwater tickles my nose, and the crashing of the waves matches the pace of my breathing.

I do not need to turn around to know what is behind me. A mid-century modern beach house, extending over the lip of the beach front's sloping bluff, looms over my shoulder. An endless expanse of blue and white sea and sky lies in front of me. I cannot see the beach or the water's edge. The bluff is too steep. I would have to descend a set of stairs if I want to reach the ocean.

"I know what has already happened here."

A sandy-colored bird with ribbed, orange legs lands on the deck, to the left of the first step extending down. "Tell me," it chirps. It looks in my direction, and I recognize the bird's hazel, watery eyes. *Dr. Patke is here to guide me, just like she said.*

"This is a summer camp, and my stepmom is one of the leaders," I intone. During my telling, I fall into the rhythm of the familiar story. "I'm in her classroom, trying to learn some important lesson. One by one, the other kids raise their hands and give her the answer she wants. But I can't figure out what to say. Eventually, she gets so mad she leaves and locks the door behind me."

Hopping on its bright feet, the bird stops next to my big toe. "Then what?"

"I break a window to escape." I stare at the broiling sea. "I'm running, hoping no one will find me. But I hear noises." In the direction of the house, muffled voices shout, and clomping boots reverberate on the wooden deck floor. "I'm being chased. I go down the steps. I stroll into the water because it looks so freeing. But before I can feel any type of weightlessness, this undercurrent grabs me. After thrashing for what feels like forever, I sink."

The bird, still standing near my toe, pecks at a feather on its wing. "What happens next?"

"I wake up, usually sweating and hurting because I've managed to injure myself again."

The tip of the bird's beak sinks into my foot. I gasp in pain and stumble backward.

"Don't tell me what happens in the waking world," the bird squawks with irritation. "What happens here?"

"Here? Well, nothing."

Behind us, the voices grow louder, and the footsteps' rumbling nears. "How do you know, dear?"

"Because I wake up."

The bird takes flight, then lands on my shoulder. Its tinny voice pierces into my eardrum. "What would happen if you didn't?"

I don't answer. Instead, I consider the possibilities. Pure terror wakes me from this dream. An old superstition is that if you die in your dreams, you die in real life. My blinding fear has always prevented me from experiencing any dream death.

I sigh. "You're saying I've been doing it wrong all this time. I'm not supposed to wake up. I'm supposed to drown."

The bird doesn't answer, just ruffles her feathers and waits. I hear the footsteps and voices a few strides behind me. I am propelled down the stairs—by my pursuers, but also by the possibility of seeing this dream through another way.

The beach is only a few feet of rocks and mud before giving way to the ocean. I do not hesitate to enter the water. Like all the times before, the anticipation of some freedom and release in the water causes my legs to skip with wide strides through the churning surf. The water's depth rises, covering my shins, then my waist and abdomen.

While distracted, I slip off the edge of an embankment. I try to turn and walk back up the bank to shallower water, but the sand under my toes slips away, and the ground beneath me disappears. I attempt to swim, but my efforts only result in the water tossing me farther from the shore. Fear replaces anticipation. The waves thunder over me. Twice, I go under the water. Choking and gasping, I fight to stay on the surface. I take one last look around, knowing with cold dread what will happen in moments.

Above me, the bird that is Dr. Patke is circling. And far, far away, perched on the edge of the horizon, there is a young man. Even though we are separated by miles upon miles of ocean, my soul connects with him.

Dormir. My fraternal twin in so many things, including gangly height and sleep diseases. He arrived on this earth with dark eyes, endless in their depths, that seem capable of pulling you into his inner core. My eyes, large and green, refract and project outward.

Dormir waves his arms, and he shouts my name over and over. I can't hear him, but I can sense his soul begging me to listen.

Listen to what? It's too late. Surely he must know that.

I go under. The last of the air empties from my lungs in a burst of bubbles. I choke, thrash, and panic. The water is nothing but frothing blackness. I know the dream is almost at its end. I am always catapulted out of the scene as the clouds of unconsciousness take over.

Something appears in the water. The bird flaps in place inches from me as effortlessly as it had flown through the air.

"Do not wake up," it twitters. "You must lucid dream, dear."

I accept the reality of this flying, talking water bird and consider its words. I knew about lucid dreaming, the act of taking control of your dreams. If I weren't already out of air, I'd laugh. I had read about lucid dreaming in books, but the feat had always sounded impossible. My nightmares encompassed every part of me. If I could control them, I would've ended them the second they started a long time ago. No one chooses to live through the terrors I face every night when I close my eyes.

"It's not impossible," the bird states. "Don't try to end the dream, Revez. Conquer it. Bend it to your will."

Bend it, but don't break it. I had never tried to lucid dream in that way.

"You can do it, Revez," the bird insists. "What does the ocean represent?"

Represents? Nothing can hold my attention, nothing but the endless water. Even when I mentally reach for my brother,

I cannot sense him. *Why does it matter?* I had tried to psychoanalyze myself before, and I had a pretty good guess as to the deeper meaning of this dream. My stepmother could never be pleased, and my attempts to escape her and find freedom would only lead to my failure.

The bird chirps in my ear, "You are strong, with or without her, Revez."

If I'm so strong, why does my attempt at finding freedom almost result in my drowning? I come to the answer as soon as I can form the question. I drown because I don't want freedom. I do not think I am capable of making it on my own.

The way to conquer the dream becomes immediately apparent. I must dispel the water.

I gather all of my panic and anticipation inside myself, then send it blasting outward.

The ocean parts around me. Waves pull backward, and the sea folds.

I cough out seawater and phlegm until my breath returns to normal. Shaking and reeling, I force myself to rise.

In front of me, a path of wet sand stretches into the horizon. The sun is rising, and the white walls of waves on either side of the road silently hold back the rest of the ocean.

With a smile, I look up. The bird circles me overhead. "Well done," it tweets. "Let us continue to the next dream world." Obediently, I follow the bird down the wave-bordered path.

To the right of me, Dormir bursts through the wave wall. He gasps and chokes. "Follow me!"

The wave splits, forming another path perpendicular to the path leading to the bird. The dream world has been split with a fine-tooth comb, its very fabric sliced by the force of Dormir's presence.

"No, do not go that way!" the furious bird squeals.

But my brother and I have always followed each other. We've always been one. I do not hesitate to step into the wave after him, allowing the water to consume me once again.

The dream crumbles. I crash into my physical body, but I am not in the office. A room of sterile white and stainless steel surrounds me. I try to move my arms, but I am tied to a metal gurney. A tightly tucked white sheet covers my naked body. My vision blurs due to a harsh lamp lowered inches from my face.

After blinking tears away, I see a metal tray suspended over my abdomen, like an overbed table used for hospital patient meals. Three objects are perched on the table: a glass of water, a piece of wood, and a brick. The water glass is turned over, and its contents dribble onto my knees.

I sense cold, clammy dampness on the back of my neck, as well. I manage to turn my head to the left, just enough to see a white towel soaked in blood. Also to my left is another gurney, and Dormir is confined to it. I can barely make out his features because his face, neck, shoulders, and every inch of visible skin not concealed by the sheet is covered in electrodes. His legs jerk, pulling against their restraints.

Standing over his constrained body is my stepmother. And next to Dormir lies Dr. Patke's still, supine body, also confined and covered in wires.

Dr. Patke coughs, then opens her eyes. "She's broken out. We connected with the brother, but he was able to tear apart the dream once he found her."

As my own weariness fades and my awareness focuses, I crinkle my face, then realize the electrodes cover every inch of my body, too.

Sheila glances at a monitor on the wall, then jerks her chin in my direction. "We must take her under again, Dr. Patke, before she fully wakes."

Dr. Patke nods. "I'm ready."

Sheila plunges a thick metal rod into the back of Dr. Patke's neck. The older woman screams, then goes still, blood pouring from the fresh wound.

Sheila hurries over to me at a brisk clip, then disappears behind me.

The heat pierces into my spine again, this time a bit lower. I wonder if it will tear through my entire body. But the heat consumes me and pulls me inward.

I am at a house party with hundreds of people. I have entered the beginning of this familiar dream. The revelers dance, drink, and grasp all over one another.

I stand in the middle of a kitchen turned dance floor. Sweaty bodies pulsate around me. They bump and sway to the bass, which vibrates the vinyl flooring underneath my feet.

In moments, gunfire will erupt. Faceless, anonymous bullets will rip through this crowd. I brace myself for the chaos. My own fear leaves me confused, and I lose control. Just like all the times before, I am an actor in this play, and the ending has already been written.

The disc jockey leans into the microphone. "Hello, Revez." The DJ stands over a pair of speakers on a corner kitchen table. The other partiers, most taller than me, create a wall between me and the table. "Remember, Revez," the DJ says, "you will win by bending the dream. Determine why this story continues to scare you, then change its ending." The amplified voice is distorted, but the crowd shifts enough for me to catch a glimpse of the figure. The DJ's hood lifts for a moment, long enough for me to glimpse a pair of watery, hazel eyes glowing in the red, pulsating lights.

I know what Dr. Patke wants me to do. *I have to lucid dream again.* I had done it once during the dream at the beach. Now, I had to find that strength inside me a second time.

As I imagine the ending of the beach dream, another thought tugs at me. A dull ache reaching down my spine reminds me that, before entering this dream, I had awakened, and I had witnessed something dreadful. *What was it?* In answer, I recall three names—Dr. Patke, Dormir, and Sheila.

"Revez!" The tone of the DJ no longer resembles Dr. Patke. Even through the distortion, I can hear the ebbs and flows of my brother's voice. "Revez, listen to me!"

The music ceases, blanketing the kitchen in sudden, invasive silence. The dancers around me complain and grumble in protest. "Hey, what happened?" one calls out.

I try to push through the crowd, but their anger plants them in place more firmly, solidifying the wall of human bodies keeping me from the DJ table.

"You have to wake up again." My brother's garbled tone speaks so quickly, I struggle to catch all the words. "They're

58

lying to you to make you complicit in their experiments. Look!"

He rips away the hood, revealing Dr. Patke's face. But it is not the warm, inviting face I remember from the sleep lab office. Her expression is twisted with selfish, merciless intent. "She's doing experiments on you, Revez! You don't have a stepmom. That's Dr. Yates! And this is Dr. Patke, who's been putting these lies in your head!"

Again, his soul reaches out to me and, this time, we link. His urgency and sincerity bring tears to my eyes. "Let me help you see the truth," he pleads.

With the connection in place and Dormir guiding me, the true reality of the beach scene unfolds. The classroom in that dream represents a lab, a lab where I could never provide the expected results. Sheila is Dr. Sheila Yates, one of the scientists who has held my brother and I captive since childhood, since before we can remember.

"Move!" I cry, but the annoyed partiers ignore me. I pull that anger inward, then release it out in a line, much as I had used to part the sea. "I said *move!*" The crowd splits as people are thrown backward, providing me with a direct view of the DJ table.

Dr. Patke wrestles with my brother for control of the microphone. Dormir tugs it toward his lips long enough to shout, "That's it, Revez! Come to me!" But Dr. Patke shoves him toward the wall with both hands. Dormir's expression shifts from hopeful to furious. The wall behind him opens, forming petals that fold outward, and sucks him into it. The wall closes behind him.

"No!" I cry. The connection between us snaps, leaving me once again alone and terrified. All goes blank, all but the dream around me. *Who was I talking to a second ago?*

Blang-blang-blang! Gunshots rip through the air. The partiers' grumbles transform to screams. Some trip over bodies already sprawled on the floor. *Blang! Blang!* A girl in front of me crumples, clutching a gaping wound in her abdomen.

I am pressed against the wall, then forced along with the tide of people as they rush toward the kitchen's exit and the house's front door.

I already know the door will not open. The unknown shooter has barricaded all the exits, trapping everyone inside. Eventually, every person in this house will be murdered. I will be the last one, and the bullet will ricochet through my skull as the dream ends.

"What does this dream represent, Revez?" Dr. Patke, hood back in place, has reclaimed the microphone. The projected voice carries to my ears even above the tortured screams of the victims. "You can't bend it until you recognize the inner fear it symbolizes."

The meaning of this scene has always seemed obvious. My crippling social anxiety and fear of crowds form this mass shooting scene, the perfect representation of the worst that could happen when confined by the worst of humanity.

To conquer this fear, I must triumph over the collective panic of this crowd. I must lead the others.

The rushing people have pushed me into the living room. The front of the line has broken at the door, forcing the victims to turn back around and creating a tangle of chaos. *Blang-blang-blang-blang!* The shooter does not need to aim because every bullet lands on some person trapped in the crowd.

The locked door shimmers. Beyond it, I see Dormir. His arms are outstretched. He is waiting to lead me to safety.

My connection to my brother is restored, and our union forms a reservoir of motivation and courage inside me. I sense that I must conquer this dream before reuniting with him. I draw upon our shared pool of strength and direct it toward my voice.

"Everyone," I cry out, "move out of the way!" My words reach their souls, just as Dormir's words had reached mine. The crowd parts, but this time due to individual choice. Even as the bullets continue to rip through the crowd members, they manage to provide me with a clear path to the exit.

With a blast of my focused, collective will, I shatter the front door to bits. Erupting into cries of relief, the people stream through the opening, and I follow them.

Outside of the house, there is only a blank, gray space. The individuals fade as soon as they run a few paces away from the front door.

Dr. Patke parts from the crowd and nods to me. "Well done, dear. One more to go." The figure touches the open space, and a portal folds open, much like the portal that took Dormir.

Beyond the portal, I see my third and final nightmare world—the mansion.

As I peer through the portal at the looming, brick structure on top of its hill, the meaning of the last dream becomes clear. In that world, the haunted mansion represents the complexities of my own inner self. I had always known I was different, and those differences frighten me.

I'm sure the final test will be to level that mansion to its foundation, knocking down its secret rooms and passages. Yet, freeing the crowd and being connected with Dormir provide me with new clarity. I am able to see my journey thus far, from beginning to end.

My own inner secrets frightened me so much that I was terrified of the outside world. And they frightened me so much that I clung to the approval of a scientist who ruthlessly experimented on me.

That scientist was Dr. Yates, who had to step down from a more active role in the experiments. My brother and I learned how to reject her attempts to invade our minds after years upon years of her torture. Now, Dr. Patke has taken her place, but their intentions are the same. They want to force something out of my brother and me, something not even we have fully grasped.

If I am ever to own every corner of myself, I have to do so outside of my dreams. I look at the hooded figure and shake my head "no," then walk around it.

"No, wait!" Dr. Patke cries, but it's too late. I release a blast of force with my left hand and open a black hole. It takes everything into it.

I open my eyes. The piece of wood on the overhead table has fallen apart into splinters. *I did that, during my dreams. Does that mean I can ...*

Dr. Patke sits up on her own gurney and begins tearing electrodes off her naked body. "Dr. Yates," Dr. Patke cries at the woman who was never my stepmother.

"Stop her! Stop her before she ruins every-thing!"

Dr. Yates sprints to my side, but she is far too slow.

Even though my brother still sleeps, I can sense his connection thrumming deep inside my soul. Everything becomes clear—Dr. Yates and Dr. Patke, after years of failure, had realized mine and my brother's abilities wouldn't manifest through force. They wanted us to see Dr. Patke as the more nurturing figure so she, when the time was right, would be allowed into the deepest recesses of our uncon-sciousnesses.

I know all of this through my re-cumbent brother's power. He can walk into other people's dreams as well as into their thoughts. This is how he communicates with me now.

As for me, my power is much more tangible. *I guess they did succeed, in a way. I am no longer afraid of my own potential.* With a flick of my eyes, I unstrap the cuffs on my wrists. I wave my index finger, and the third object on the table, the brick, crumbles into dust.

Electrodes tear away from my skin. I sit up. Dr. Yates and Dr. Patke stare at me, slack-jawed and horrified.

Pop-pop-pop. All of the intravenous needles explode out of my veins. Then, I re-direct their dripping, shining points at the two women, coiling them back toward me like snakes.

"What will you do to us?" Dr. Patke gasps.

"I think that's implied, don't you?"

I let my wrists drop, and the needles plunge toward their fleshy targets.

SHELLY X LEONN'S BIO

Shelly's the author of The Broken Series. After graduating w/ a Bachelor of Arts in journalism, Shelly worked at her hometown newspaper as the web & youth editor. During her time advising the youth staff, Shelly realized her true calling was teaching. Her years in educ. were spent in middle & high school language arts classrooms. She is now an adjunct professor and a development manager committed to amplifying the voices of marginalized youth. She & her two boys reside in Affton, & she enjoys reading, writing, outdoor activities, anime, video games, & other dorky pastimes.

https://www.instagram.com/shellyxleonnauthor/

LIKE THE PRESENT by

Amanda Lance

<u>February 14th</u>
Something happened today.

I don't even know *how* to explain it. But I guess that doesn't matter since the whole thing was a dream anyway. No other explanation for it.

I'll admit it though: I'm worried. I've never fallen asleep in class before. Not even last year when I was doing all those extracurriculars on top of babysitting and Meals on Wheels and all that other crap to bulk up the college applications. Ugh.

So, for me to just randomly fall asleep in class now? What the hell? Not to mention that dream…it creeps me out thinking about it. Don't think I've ever had one that felt *that* real.

Shit. I thought I could keep my GPA while working (more or less) full-time at Pete's, but maybe I need a break. A day or two off. Would be nice to come home and not have to scrub the smell of pepperoni off my skin. I swear that on-ion/garlic smell seeps straight into my pores.

Maybe it's got nothing to do with work and school. I just need to start taking better care of myself—start eating tree bark or whatever Kate is always on about. Ha! Wouldn't she just love that?

February 15th

I'm not looking forward to college.

It sounds…wrong?

Everyone I know who's going is excited about it. Freaking thrilled.

Guess that's why I don't even feel comfortable writing it—forget about say-ing it out loud. I'm only eighteen, but the world expects me to know what I want to do with my life. How am I supposed to *know* if college is what I should be doing?

I have no *reason* to complain. I've got it much better than other people. I'm young and healthy. I've got decent parents and Kate is okay as far as big sisters go.

Something is missing. I have this hollow pit in me. Feels like it gets a bit deeper every day.

February 16th
Me, Mom and Dad met Kate's new girlfriend today. We went to some vegan place Kate likes, so of course they didn't serve *anything* edible. At least the girl-friend seems nice enough. Her name is Bexley. Not much of a talker so instant thumbs-up in my book.

The "food" was awful, but the company was lovely, and it was nice to see

Kate all doe-eyed and shit. I wasn't happy though and I can't even really say why.

I laughed when everybody else laughed. Nodded at appropriate times. Kate looked at me funny a couple of times but didn't mention it. I wouldn't have talked about it even if she had. Cause the thing is that I didn't feel *unhappy* either. Didn't feel much at all. It reminded me of when I got my wisdom teeth taken out. There was a hint of pain around the edges but mostly I was just numb.

It wasn't a bad sensation, just weird. Lots of things have been weird the last few weeks.

February 18th
It happened again today.

It was in study hall this time. I was attempting to finish some homework, but a gaggle of girls nearby wouldn't shut up.

Other people were watching videos on their phone—volume high. Someone else was popping gum and another guy only had one earbud in. As if the rest of us wanted to hear the heavy metal he was listening to. The teacher in charge didn't care enough to tell anyone to be quiet.

I couldn't concentrate. Everyone's voices got louder but not just that—they got all mixed up, turned to static. It didn't just give me a headache, it felt like my brain was vibrating. Like it was trying to shake itself out of my head.

I tried taking deep breaths.

It didn't help. If anything, the noise got louder—the static of everything was eating away at my eardrums like a parasite or something. All I wanted in the world at that moment was for it to stop. Stop. Stop. STOP!

It stopped.

Everything stopped.

It was perfectly silent. No lockers slamming in the hallway. No squeaky desk chairs or wrappers crinkling. No more static.

The girl closest to me, her mouth was open. Totally still. Another's face was crinkled mid-sneeze. Some other girl's hair was suspended mid-air as she flipped it. There were over a dozen people and they were like…statues! A memorial to young idiots. Ha!

I want to say I didn't freak out, but I did. I fell off the bench I was sitting on. I stood up and ran to the hallway for help but saw a custodian immobile with one leg lifted in stride.

Back inside study hall, I shook people by their shoulders. I called their names and waved my hands in front of their faces.

Then it occurred to me: phone! Duh! Emergency! Call for help!

My hands shook as I got my phone out of my back pocket, but I couldn't get it to work. Every button I pressed did nothing. A member of the gaggle had her phone stuck in her hand, so I pried it from her fingers.

I read the time:
1:23PM
Guess what? Her phone wouldn't do anything either.

I checked three others at random and left them in a pile at the front of the room.

By then I couldn't catch my breath and my upper lip was sweating. I had no idea what to do.

I went back to my bench and kicked off my shoes before resting my head in my hands.

I had a theory then. Maybe this was a dream within a dream or something. Some Leonardo DiCaprio nonsense. Maybe I'd wake up when I fell asleep in my dream. I closed my eyes: clenched them really. I concentrated on waking up. Wake up. Wake up. Wake up!

Everything turned back on.

It was like a switch flipped. *Everything* started back up again. The girl finished sneezing, guys kept chewing, girls kept laughing…

I know it wasn't real. It couldn't be real.

But why were my shoes off when I woke up?

How could I watch a bunch of people get confused as they looked for their phones—eventually finding them where I'd left them…in my dream?

More evidence it was real: I still had my phone in hand. It was turning 1:24PM.

All the stuff that happened: everything stopping, me freaking out, trying to use the phones, it all went down in a single minute?

But it was a *dream* minute, right? None of it was real.

It couldn't have been.
Right?

February 18th (Later…)

Okay, I've thought about it. Some of this stuff is explainable.

1. I *did* fall asleep. Don't think it's ever happened with my eyes open before, but I looked it up, and it is a thing.
2. While I was asleep, I kicked off my shoes. Just like tossing and turning. Totally possible.

Not sure how to explain the other stuff, including the forming bruise on my ass from when I fell off the bench.

I'm chalking up the time thing to coincidence. It's not likely that I dreamed about the exact time but it's not impossible.

The only other thing I can come up with is that I **stopped time**…which makes me feel half-crazy just writing it.

2/24

I'm not crazy.

It seems important to write that down, so I'll do it again.

I am not crazy.

It was just like earlier this week. Only this time, it was no dream. It wasn't any of the other times either, but I know for sure now:

I stopped time.

Time! Stopped it! Me!
Holy shit!

Here's what went down:

I'm working at Pete's, and we're busy as usual. I'll spare the details but, basically, some drunk guy came in and started harassing Kera. I don't even like her but even my inner feminist was getting annoyed. Worst part? No one was doing anything about it!

On top of that, the phone wouldn't stop ringing and my feet hurt. I had five people on hold and a line of huffy people demanding their orders. There was just so much noise, noise, noise!

Like the last time, all I could think was how I wanted it to stop, stop, stop!

That was all it took. Everything stopped. Again.

This time I didn't freak out. Might as well make the most of this, right?

I noted that the time was 6:48PM and grabbed some ice from the freezer. I then went over to the guy who'd been making comments about Kera's posterior for the last half-hour and proceeded to jam said ice down the front of his pants.

Time restarted soon after, and the first thing I heard was a grown man squealing (loudly) about the cold. He grabbed his crotch—there were sounds of general disgust all around—but when people could see that the fabric was wet, the place erupted with laughter.

The guy was so embarrassed he basically tried to run out of there and almost fell on his face when he did. Serves him right.

Again, I watched the final seconds of 6:48PM click away on the novelty wall clock. I swear that tacky pizza-shaped clock had never been more beautiful.

2/25

Stayed up all night doing research. Got to school late but don't think anybody noticed. Turns out the idea of stopping time isn't a new one. All theories seem to include traveling at the speed of light. Looking up formulas now.

2/26

Skipped school to conduct experiments. Reading online. Lot of books published about gambling/stopping time. Got some online. Need to go to library.

I haven't been able to stop or start time with control. I'd like to be able to do it quickly, without thinking. Muscle memory. The ability seems connected to my emotions, especially anger. Further experimentation required.

2/26 (Later…)

I forgot Kate and I were supposed to go shopping for Dad's birthday present today. The arrangement involved picking me up from school. My parents learned I wasn't there. Told Mom I'd been sick. I looked crappy enough that she believed me. Kate apologized for getting snippy at me. Offered to get me soup from the Jewish deli.

Almost wanted to tell her what was going on. She wouldn't get it. I don't have the energy to explain.

2/28? 3/1?
Hypothesis #9 has proven correct. Stopping time is related to emotional state.
Walking to library and heard screaming. Saw a kid falling from a tree. One of those decorative trees planted in the middle of the sidewalk. It was a good six-foot fall off ground and the kid was going to land face-first. Instinctively scared for her. When time stopped, I crossed the street. Took her by the arms. Set her straight on her feet.

She probably only would've lost some teeth. Baby teeth. Maybe would've

broken her nose. The incident made me realize my purpose. College isn't what I'm
supposed to be doing—helping people is. I
don't think I'm supposed to be a superhero
or anything. Just make the world slightly
less crappy.

All those hollow places in me are
filled up. It feels good.

I feel good.

3/3?

Conclusion for Experiment #17:
Natural elements (water, fire, wind) are
only subjected to time control when in my
immediate presence. Exact distance unknown.

March 10th

I've explained it all a dozen times
now, but this accounting will be the last
one. I'm not mad at them for not believing
me—can't say I'd believe me either if I
were them—but I did finally realize that I
have to lie if I want to get out of here. One

of those smile, nod and keep your mouth shut situations.

"Of course, I must have been delusional. Of course, the incident at Dad's birthday party didn't really happen."

So, three days ago it was Dad's birthday party. Only about thirty people. Nothing special, really. It was everything you'd expect from a lower-middle class family: dollar-store tablecloths, empty beer cans all over, kids double-dipping in the salsa…

My point is that the entire thing was very normal. There were no warning signs. Not really. In hindsight, I think Mom's cooking covered up the smell. Really, that's the only thing it could have been. Between the sausage and pepper, ziti, everybody probably only smelled garlic. If they *did* smell the propane, they probably took one look at the tray of deviled eggs and assumed it was that. Maybe they thought someone just farted. Who knows?

About two hours into the thing, I escaped by going down to the basement. Told Mom I'd grab more bottles of water.

I was there for five minutes when Bex came down the stairs. She teased me for hiding down there but asked if she could join me. Said one of my uncles kept trying to get her to pull his finger. So yeah. Fine. Sure. Why not?

But then Bex pulls out a pack of cigarettes from her bag. She asks me not to tell my sister.

As I watch her put the cigarette in her mouth, I saw the air sort of shimmer…

I blinked. Looked closer. I realized what it was, but Bex already had her lighter out.

I screamed "STOP!" *for* Bex not to flick her lighter but it was time that paused instead.

It was a leak. A gas leak!

My heart was beating so fast it **hurt**. Felt like that one time I tried to run in high school.

There was a paused explosion erupting from the furnace. It was on the other side of the basement and only a second into forming, but the heat from it was searing.

I grabbed one of Dad's toolboxes and shut off all the gas valves in the house. He taught Kate and I how to do this for THIS EXACT REASON. Made us go over it a bunch of times when we were kids. I've never been so thankful for his nagging.

While I did it, I thought about Mom directly above the furnace with the stove on. She and anyone else in the kitchen would have been goners. Everybody in the living room/dining room would have died too. Whoever was in the bathroom might have been okay, but the house would have collapsed for sure. At a minimum, anyone upstairs would have been hurt badly.

Naturally, I went for the fire extinguisher under the kitchen sink, but the nitrogen and dry foam were trapped inside, stuck on pause like the other elements. Instead, I had to put out the flames with three giant boxes of baking soda.

Side note: I swear I'll never give Mom a hard time for buying in bulk ever again.

Things got weird after that—*weirder*. When the adrenaline crash came, I must have fallen asleep. Maybe fainted from the stress? Whatever. When I woke up, I was here. Not *here*, specifically but downstairs in the ER where a doctor with tuna breath was shining a light in my eyes. Mom and Kate were there with dried tear tracks on their faces, asking me if I was okay.

And because I am the biggest idiot on the planet, I told them what happened.

Mom started crying. Me, being a bit out of it, thought she was crying out of relief. I tried to reassure her, explain everything, but she only cried harder.

The hospital staff took my blood and looked for brain tumors and when all that stuff came back negative, my family accepted what the doctors told them. They said I had a psychotic break. That I've been hallucinating all this time. They said I'm sick. There's been talk of schizophrenia. There's been pamphlets and repeated phrases like "recent erratic behavior is common upon onset."

There has been a lot of pills.

I know that's not true, of course, but I understand why they think that. My family isn't like me. They can't see what I see.

They tell a story of me going to the basement and not coming back. Bex finding me sitting on the floor; not moving, not talking, staring at nothing. Kate called 911 when she saw I'd wet myself. Mom cried to the paramedics about the family history of strokes.

I was…asleep, I guess? Comatose from exerting my abilities like that. I wasn't aware of any of it.

Later, the doctor told my parents I had been in a catatonic state.

It makes sense, I admit. I even questioned my own sanity for a minute. But if I really am crazy, then how did I know about the gas leak? When did the basement get doused with baking soda?

In the chaos, the party obviously ended, and Dad realized the smell wasn't just coming from the line for the bathroom. A firefighter who came with the paramedics found the shut off valves…the leak…eventually the entire street got evacuated. The gas company came and fixed everything, so no one was hurt. A happy ending for all. Except for one little detail:

I haven't been able to stop time since.

I don't know if it's the medicine they're giving me (it makes me super drowsy) or something else.

I have a theory that my gift was a temporary one—something I was only supposed to use for the specific purpose of saving my family. Maybe now that I've achieved that, I've lost my abilities.

Then again, maybe I just need to get out of here. Away from these pills.

And like I said, I've given up on convincing the staff or my family about this.

The doctor and the therapist offer an explanation by telling me I might have been *subconsciously* aware of the leak.

They won't hear anything other than what they *want* to hear. I don't argue anymore.

Instead, I'm being polite, keeping my head down and my mouth shut, taking the medication without complaint. Anything to go home. Get back to helping people. Being useful. Until then?

I'm just biding my time.

AMANDA LANCE'S BIO

Amanda Lance is a dedicated bookworm with work published by institutions such as Limitless Publishing, The Wild Rose Press, and Elephantine Publishing. Amanda holds an MFA in Creative Writing as well as an MA in Liberal Studies. She currently resides in Pennsylvania with her husband and three dogs.

https://www.instagram.com/authoramandalance/

SUN BURN by LL Montez

The welcome center was smaller than expected. It was a compact waiting room with a beige front desk and a neglected plant in the corner. A few scuffed-up terracotta-colored plastic chairs lined the wall of windows that looked out into the star-littered galaxy beyond. Priyank distracted herself from her anxiousness by tracing the ancient etchings on the tungsten floor until her number appeared in the boxy display above the front desk.

"Number four-hundred and sixteen," the elderly gentleman behind the counter called.

Priyank stood. When sitting, it was hard to tell that they were rotating. Standing was a different story.

The black metal floor rotated slowly enough for the young dignitary to keep her balance until the ancient etchings in the metal floor caught her heel. She wobbled, righting herself to keep from falling.

Thunderous heat roared from the black double-doors across the room. She clutched her yellow legal pad with her people's pleas close to her chest. In her heart, she carried their tears pouring over their fruitless land, their unending funeral dirges sung from the empty center of their prominent ribs yawning over concave middles. Priyank wrapped herself in their agony to keep momentum toward the Sun. It had to realize that it was causing distress—the Sun would help where it could, she was sure.

"Number four-hundred and sixteen, sir," she said.

The elderly man in a smart suit and bowtie looked up from his work. "How can I help you today?"

Priyank stepped up to his desk. "I'm here to speak to the Sun. I have an appointment."

Without another word, the man returned his focus to his desk. He left her to squirm in place as she used all her will-power to not look over the counter and see what was occupying him. Did she say something wrong?

"Please write your name here—" without looking up, he slapped a blank, white sticker and pen on the counter be-tween them. Twisting in his swivel chair, he gestured toward the black double-doors be-hind him, "—and enter when you're ready."

With the sticker against her blazer and its discarded back crumpled in her sweaty hand, she faced the massive black doors. The door mirrored the same ancient scribblings on the rotating floor. She had memorized their lines and curves as she waited to be called but had no idea what they meant. Could be an ominous warning. Could be a warm welcome. Could be an old recipe for a favorite flavor of pie, but she might never know.

Clutching her notepad closer, she shut her eyes and stepped forward. The doors opened for her.

The Sun, or at least the slice that was visible to guests, gargled fire behind the enormous black window of the cavernous room. The inky darkness of the Sun's room was a stark contrast to the painful fluorescence of the reception area. The tinted window veiled the Sun's arching spurts in muted orange. Its muffled roar shook the room as another flare whipped out and struck the barrier between them.

Run, said every instinct she possessed.

Priyank held her notepad tighter, crushing the pages against her chest. No. She had a job to do.

The shadows stirred beside her. A dark arch reflected black sunlight as if one of the Sun's violent flares had broken through the glass.

Priyank stumbled back, crushing her notepad between her arms and chest. She curled inward, waiting for the fiery whip to smack her down, but she stood her ground. "I have an appointment!"

Nothing hit her. When figuring it was safe to peek around her crumpled notepad, she saw that the flare was a guy--a handsome guy around her age. When he stepped in closer, she was transfixed by the sheen of sweat across his dark, bare chest and the glimmer of the slick material of his black shorts that hugged every muscle of his thighs. Priyank hid behind her notepad again.

"Welcome to the Sun Room. My name is Knue. I'll be your interpreter today." He waved at her. "What's your question?"

"I didn't know I needed an interpreter."

His smile flashed bright white. "It's a free service."

Not to be distracted by his near nakedness, Priyank cleared her throat. She tugged the ends of her navy blazer down and squared her shoulders. "I've come as a delegate from my planet. My people are suffering, and I would like to begin negotiations."

Knue's smile faded before he turned his back to her to face the Sun.

"No! Wait. I demand we begin negotiations," she said before he could begin his translation.

Knue tilted his head, his ear toward her.

She raised her chin and flipped the first page of her legal pad over to read her notes. "Six orbits ago, without warning, explanation, or apology, the Sun moved away from my planet, and I am here to negotiate a plan to return it to its original location so that our planet can thrive again."

She couldn't ignore the hitch of hesitation in the outline of Knue's practically naked body before he turned to address the Sun.

"I have with me more than three-hundred-thousand complaints from individuals and communities of my planet ranging from extreme famine, receding coastlines, eternal winters, and death by starvation to crippling conditions caused by vitamin D deficiencies." Priyank flipped through some of her pages to quote the direst grievances.

"Okay, okay." Knue held his hand up. He smiled, but not with the same brilliance as before. "One problem at a time."

Knue clapped his hands once. From within his palms, a white light buzzed to life. He rubbed them together, kinetic energy crackling between them as smokey heat unfurled from between his fingers. A ribbon of yellow light ran the circumference of his head like a halo. Strands of daybreak beamed from under his long feet. He dropped to the floor, lying flat, crossing his arms palm-down on his chest. The light from his soles streamed from him like two flashlights in the dark.

Priyank couldn't tear her eyes away from him this time. He had become more radiant than the Sun she knew. She parted her lips to question him, but a rumble threw her off-kilter.

A slow, pounding beat emitted from the Sun behind the glass as if it was turning its focus to Knue. The deep rhythm vibrated against the metal floor. It spurred Knue to burst up, lifting his

leg and arching his body to stand as if he was the curl of a solar flare. Light streamed from his flat palms as he circled his muscular arms around his body, twisting his torso and bending low to sweep the lights across the floor. He leaped into the air, the band across his head blinking like slow, tired eyes while his body contracted and billowed for the Sun in a tribal dance.

He stopped and faced the window.

Priyank blinked, her mouth agape. With all her might, she wished he would dance again. "That was--"

The Sun's response was a blast of fire flicking in their direction and away.

Knue turned to face Priyank. He held his hands and their beams behind his back before standing tall and translating. "There will be no negotiation."

All thoughts of the beautiful dance fled her mind as Priyank squeezed the legal pad between her hands. "Why not?"

Knue bit his bottom lip. His hands ignited again as he lifted his arm and brought it down as a waving arc. He glided across the floor on his knees, the rays spinning from his feet.

The Sun burped another string of fire.

"There is nothing to do. You insult me for thinking you could move the universe on a plea. You must leave." Knue shrugged with palms out, mouthing an apology.

"No!" Priyank didn't travel this far and long for a three-minute shut-down with the Sun. She didn't ditch her family on their

101

deathbeds to be brushed aside. "You can't send me away! You're killing my people."

Knue was about to move, but she continued.

"Give me just a few years of stronger reach." She ran up to the glass separating them and pounded it with her fist. Crushed pages from her legal pad fanned out from her clutches like Knue's rays. "Just a few good summers to help us learn to live without you."

Behind her, Knue spun, the beams in his palms blazing. He spread his fingers wide, pointing his glowing palms away from his eyes. He reached up like a bolt of lightning. He launched himself from the ground, his arms and legs stretching in different directions as he kicked out the light from under him. Pirouetting, he lifted his left foot to arc a strand of sunshine around the room.

The Sun didn't respond.

"You're going to let an entire planet die," she screamed, dropping to her knees, her pad and ripped papers falling to her side.

Knue leaped behind her, thrusting his hands and lights out above his head. He rattled the platform as he landed, stomping out the beams under his feet.

A heavy knock at the door behind Priyank echoed through the chamber. She flinched, startled at the reminder that there were others waiting on an audience with the Sun too.

Knue was at her side. "The Sun has another appointment waiting. I'm sorry."

"No!" She screamed at the glass, smashing the papers against it so the Sun could read her people's desperate pleas for itself. "I don't accept that answer. You owe us an explanation. Why did you leave? You need to come back and let my people live again."

Knue didn't move. The Sun responded on its own. It built an enormous boil of fire against its surface and lashed out at the black glass under Priyank's hand. A ringing crack echoed

through the room, breaking the glass. Squeezing through the tiny aperture, a whip of solar cord struck out and slashed Priyank across her cheek She cried out, ducking and covering her head with her hands in case the sun lashed out again.

"I have heard enough from you. Everyone must accept what they are given. That is the way it's done. Take this mark as a warning." Knue's warm hands held her shoulders as he attempted to quell her shaking. "My next appointment is waiting."

With one hand over her cheek and the other feeling out for the scattered pages of the legal pad on the ground around her, Priyank choked down the desire to lean into Knue and cry on his shoulder. "This can't be the end."

He let her lean on him.

Tears slid down her cheeks as the sting from her burned skin was overtaken by the agony of realizing she'd have to re-turn home without a solution. "I promised everyone I'd succeed. I promised everyone that the Sun would listen, and everything would be okay. I can't go back like this."

Knue slipped his arm around her shoulder as he led her toward the double doors. That was all he needed to say.

At the doors, she paused. The brightness of the waiting room streamed behind her, fully revealing his kind face. A myriad of pale scars criss-crossed his cheeks and forehead. Priyank's gaze fol-lowed the trail of burns down his neck, shoulders, arms, hands, and torso. They were exact replicas of the one the Sun had given her for talking back.

"Keep trying," he said. When he leaned into the light, his scars caught the shine of the office's garish bulbs. "It seems impossible, and it will feel impossible for a really long time, but the Sun can change its mind."

"Did it hurt?" Her finger hovered over the new line down her face.

"It still does."

Priyank reached out to touch his scars, but stopped when she thought he might find her

curiosity rude. "What was so important that you let the Sun beat you up like that?"

Knue gazed down at her. He shifted his weight from one foot to the other. "Because I was

sent on a mission by my planet to find a way to save us from our impending doom." Priyank's knees buckled.

He rested his head against the doorframe. "I needed the Sun to inch a little closer to my planet or else everyone on it would die."

The Sun had moved away from her people because of Knue.

Frosty dread crept its way up her bones. Priyank gathered the loose papers in her hands and realigned them with the top of her legal pad. She smoothed out the crumpled page as best she could. "Then I guess I'll be seeing you again really soon."

LL MONTEZ' BIO

LL Montez is a Mexican-American writer raised on the savage Chicago streets. Her debut manuscript, ARC10, won a Wattpad 2017 Watty Storysmith award for "mastery of style, plot, and character development" from among 280,000 entries. As co-host of The WritersXL — a podcast helping writers through their publishing journeys — she shares her joy and writing acumen with all who dare to tune in for an hour of irreverent banter and writing advice. When not writing or podcasting about writing, she recruits fertility healthcare professionals, reads tarot cards on the full moon, boxes for fun, performs bizarre sci-fi stories at local occult bookstores, and practices her abuela's brujeria with her husband, daughter, and dog at her side.

https://www.llmontez.com/

STAR CATCHER by Stephanie

Hansen

Once the universe stopped expanding, it began to crumple back in. This happened at the peak of the world and, instead of continuing forward, history began to repeat itself in reverse. To know what happens next, to have a crystal ball had once been a desired thing but no more. It was now a condemnation, an inescapable jail sentence, a curse. There was, though, another possibility, a glitch in the system, but it had yet to be discovered. Until Exeri found it, or so she thought.

  When she failed to save Crostina from death, it was soul crushing, heart shattering, and breath stopping. She could remember the first time they'd met. Crostina had a habit of calling people out. She set aside societal politeness in an effort to save everyone from emotional pain. Populations had formed bad habits that left them so far from agreement, amity had become a forgotten thing.

The look Crostina had given the star catcher in training was to die for. She could make someone pee their pants in fear with that look.

"So I have to fly around it to change the gravity?" the star catcher had asked.

"Seriously, you just went through months of aviation boarding school training." Crostina rolled her eyes.

"I'm just checking," said the star catcher.

"How'd you even pass?" Crostina asked.

"Whatever. It's not like you're going out there to wrangle a star," the star catcher replied.

That's when it happened. She gave him the look, and he froze right there.

Exeri walked up beside him with the biggest grin on her face. Crostina looked at Exeri, shook her head side to side, and handed the baffled student a ship key. He proceeded to open his mouth to say something else so Exeri interrupted.

"Oh, hey, are you…" Exeri looked at his name tag. "Vincent?"

"Yeah," he replied.

"The captain asked me to give you a message."

This stopped him. Then he turned to Exeri. "What's the message?"

"The captain said you need to meet her on hangar three."

With that, Vincent's eyes got huge. He turned, and speed walked away.

"You know hangar three is out of commission right now," Crostina commented with another one of her gorgeous death stares. Her eyes shined like sand glittering in the sun.

"Well, he doesn't seem to know that, and it got him out of your hair," Exeri said.

Crostina ever so slightly smirked with the response. It was the hidden

111

beginnings of a smile that snagged Exeri. A piece of Exeri's heart would always be Crostina's from then on.

"How can I help you?" Crostina asked, noticing that Exeri's dark, curly hair had runaway star infrared like waves.

Forming any words had been extremely difficult. Exeri cleared her throat and attempted to utter a coherent sentence.

"Would you like to take a break and go for a walk on the deck?"

Then Exeri was hit with a thousand bolts of lightning as Crostina issued a broad, beaming smile.

"Actually, that sounds perfect."

Between flights when the dome was in place, they'd been allowed to stroll the deck. During their walk the sky was unlit in some places and billowing with bright, rainbow tinted clouds everywhere else. The brilliant stars around them seemed within reach which felt fitting given the space station's purpose. The shortage of energy at home had driven people to alternatives.

112

One of those being stars. Exeri had felt compelled to sign up at once. The thought of lassoing a star drew her in, but she'd never expected to be caught herself by a miraculous cataclysm of cosmic dust.

To Exeri's utter amazement, Crostina seemed to return her feelings, for she clung to her arm as they made their way, avoiding the hangars. Part of her kept waiting for the other shoe to drop, for Crostina to make up an excuse to leave, but it never happened.

"This was exactly what I needed. Thank you for suggesting it," Crostina exclaimed.

"I didn't realize until I saw you, but it was just what I needed too."

"What do you think goes through a star's mind before it's caught?"

"Well, let's see, with gravity taken out of balance, the forceful nature takes over. I'd wager its last thought might be one of anger."

That walk had been the beginning of Exeri's greatest journey. She had traversed across the universe in search of answers and, while there had been many adventures, she'd always been a bit lost. Until she found her gravitational lodestar in Crostina, she'd been spinning out of control.

***

Now traveling backward, Exeri could remember all of this background as well as the heartache she'd felt when she lost Crostina. You see, there had been a reason why Crostina had given the star catcher in training such a look of reproach. A year previously Crostina had retired from teenage chasing stars after a close call with a wolf ship. Balance had to be maintained when using star energy, but the wolf crew wanted it for themselves no matter how out of balance it brought the system.

The particular wolf crew that crossed paths with Crostina had been extra cutthroat but still no match for the beautiful girl with a death stare. She looped around them as if they were as slow as slugs. Their counter moves did the opposite of what they'd planned. Before too long, she'd caused them to be flung out of control, far into space, and nowhere near the gaseous ball they'd sought. The act had also thrown Crostina into such a tailspin that her adrenaline had spiked and her breath had grown rapid. Simply put, it had knocked the wind out of her and ended her pilot days.

About nine months after Crostina had won Exeri's heart and, at a time when the deck had been empty save one catcher ship, it just so happened that was also the time that a call came in reporting of another rogue wolf crew. Only one person had been there to take it. So back in the pilot seat Crostina had gone and, from that moment on and back, Exeri planned and plotted how to change that moment in time. She had failed to save Crostina then, but she would not let it happen again. All she had to figure out was how to do it backward.

"Exeri, report your location," Captain Hughes requested.

The sound of mostly silence but a bit of static was all that came back over the radio. Exeri was leagues away in search of a certain wolf crew. In her time moving forward, she had investigated for years until she had found the identities of the individuals involved. The problem was that once she'd figured it out, time no longer moved forward. Now she could do more than seek revenge. In the new pattern she could try to save her love instead.

***

The wolf captain's name was Mills Benard, and he was leagues away, bossing around his first officer, Charles Dugan.

"I don't care if they shut it down," Benard yelled at Dugan. "I want that sector. It's star rich."

"There's too much risk. It's constantly patrolled."

"Ah. Come on, I thought you loved a challenge."

"I like a good challenge, but you're looking at chasing a royal flush against a pocket pair…no…worse."

"I'm looking at winning the universal lottery, pal," Benard patted Dugan on the back.

Dugan sighed loudly while his shoulders drooped.

"Ah, you're still upset about that run in!"

"It wasn't just a run in. That catcher died, man."

The pair were currently based on Planet Funen, the place of relics. They were standing around a rectangle table covered in felt holding pool sticks. It could have seemed like Earth if it weren't for the alien fog visible through the sky light. The fog seemed to be alive with curling fingers of smoke.

Dugan's face had gone pale as an aged cucumber, yellow instead of green, as he recalled watching the catcher's ship go far beyond control and explode. Sure, he'd grown up poor and, therefore, had a different opinion on stealing than the general population but to be the cause of another's death, that was incomprehensible.

"They know the risk when they sign up just as you do, son."

Benard was like a father to Dugan, but Dugan was on the verge of late onset teenage rebellion.

***

The chances of Exeri discovering this information were slim to none, but it just so happened that Captain Hughes was in the very same bar. With the smell of chalk and bourbon swirling around her, Captain Hughes' ears perked up when she heard 'that catcher died' from behind where she sat.

The day the star catchers lost Crostina had been one of the worst in Captain Hughes' tenure. Crostina had been like a daughter to her. Through training, she had seen herself in the girl. There was grit where in others weakness belonged.

Crostina caught on quick and had more heart than she'd seen before in a student. It took every piece of control she had not to beat up the two jerks right then and there, but she wouldn't stoop to their insulting low level. She planned to turn them into the authorities. Slightly pivoting to exit, Captain Hughes engaged her eyepiece to secure the audio in addition to visual recording of their conversation with her ear microphone chip.

Back at the satellite hotel away from the noise, Captain Hughes opened a line of communication with the authorities while Exeri lay in the opposite bed.

"Hello?" the captain asked.

The sound stirred Exeri.

"Yes, I need to report a theft and human slaughter," the captain continued.

Exeri rubbed her eyes.

"No, it didn't just happen."

Exeri sat up.

"You're going to transfer me to a different department?"

Exeri cut the connection.

"Hey!" Captain Hughes yelled.

"What are you yammering about? I was asleep"

"It's nothing."

"No, no, I heard you say human slaughter. What human slaughter?"

Captain Hughes sat on the made bed and heaved a sigh. "You know what human slaughter, Exeri."

Exeri's jaw dropped, and a tear threatened to fall from her eye.

"You found them?"

"Yes."

Captain Hughes played the recordings for Exeri.

***

Within a day, Exeri had pulled every string she could and secured two interstellar bounty hunters to track down the wolf crew members from Captain Hughes' footage.

"That's like finding a needle in a haystack," one investigator had said.

120

"Oh, come on, I'm sure you know where the wolf crews hang out."

That's when it hit Exeri. She couldn't believe she hadn't thought of it before. Every night for the next two months she was at the bar on Planet Funen hustling the pool table.

She was there so much that she'd memorized the regulars' drinks, the bartender's habits, and knew who the best server was. She'd about given up when the pair from Captain Hughes' recordings walked through the door.

Strolling to the galaxy jukebox, she eyed them the entire way. Then she moved to the bar while the two men played a game of pool. After a few moments of watching the game to its conclusion, she approached the players and challenged the winner.

"Bet I can take you," she told the younger of the two.

"Oh yeah?" The burly man said. "It's on."

As she racked, she kept envisioning the older man saying, "You still upset about that run in?" and the anger grew like an unforgiving, cancerous tumor inside her.

Every time a pool stick hit a ball, her anger rose until, finally, she couldn't take it anymore. As the older man was leaning over a high-top table, she put her hand on the back of his head and smashed his face down. Then she did it again and again until blood splattered.

After recovering from the shock of what he was seeing, Dugan appeared to help Benard. "Stop! What are you doing? Stop!"

Exeri tried adopting Crostina's look. She wanted to make Dugan piss his pants with a death stare. It didn't work, so she punched him in the throat instead. As he fell to the ground, she returned to Benard and punched him in the gut. When he fell backward and lay on the ground. Exeri pulled out her radiation gun.

"No! Stop," Dugan gasped out as he crawled over to Benard. He put his body on top of the older man, acting as a shield.

In that moment, for a split second, Exeri no longer saw a murderer in front of her. It was like rain washing away a chalk drawing on cement. The ugliness she had viewed in the man disappeared. This shift seemed to also happen in a larger sense.

For some reason, the reversal of time had caused a uniform effect in people. All across the universe, people everywhere seemed to recognize errors and see beauty they hadn't seen before. In that second, time didn't move forward, and it was no longer in reverse. For a moment, time stood still. But Exeri didn't pull the trigger.

"Why should I let him live? Why should I let you live? You killed my love."

Recognition came across the man's face. "Wait, you're…? It was…?" he fumbled.

"Yes, the star catcher you caused to die," Exeri yelled. "I loved her."

"That moment still haunts me," Dugan said.

"Would you change it if you could?" Exeri asked.

Benard moaned.

"Yes, but how?"

"Stop stealing stars," Exeri said.

"But we need them," Dugan insisted.

Benard pushed away from Dugan and sat up with a scowl on his face.

"Don't talk to government employees, Dugan," Benard moaned out while touching his face, assessing the wounds.

Exeri rolled her eyes at Benard. "Right, because partnering with criminals is so much better than talking to a government employee."

"I've been around a lot longer than you," Benard said with asperity. "I've seen ten times more better hearts out of criminals than anyone from the government."

"Oh, so that makes it okay to kill star catchers," Exeri said.

"You don't seem to give a second thought to killing people you've never met."

"We don't usually kill anyone."

"Sure didn't seem like that when you had your radiation gun," Dugan said.

For a moment Exeri was able to visualize how she looked standing over them full of rage. She lowered the weapon and sat in a chair with a huff.

"What if I could warn you where the star catchers are so you could avoid run ins?" Exeri asked.

Benard actually began to smile but then brushed it off. "How could we trust you?"

"We don't want anyone hurt at all," Dugan claimed.

And so it went, Exeri, Dugan, and Benard worked to establish a partnership so no star catchers and no wolf crew members would be hurt again. Something about this accord seemed to spread throughout the universal population. A snowball effect occurred as more and more worked to-gether. The universe began expanding again.

***

With a night sky behind them as the squadron ship glided through space, Exeri walked with Crostina's hand in hers. They stopped, and Exeri grabbed Crostina's other hand so they were facing each other. They became lost in one another's eyes, knowing to treasure every moment. A shooting star blazed over the dome and Crostina smiled her beaming smile. Exeri kissed the beauti-ful woman with the death stare. It was a kiss she never thought she'd ever have again. She was over the moon; head over heels with Crostina.

"Get a room, you two," Captain Hughes barked.

"Leave them be," Vincent said.

Captain Hughes laughed and patted him on the back. "All right! How about we go fix hangar three?"

"Really?" Vincent asked.

Crostina and Exeri watched the two walk away. In that moment everything felt right. They hoped it would last forever.

STEPHANIE HANSEN'S BIO

Stephanie Hansen's debut novel, *Replaced Parts*, released this year with Fire & Ice YA and Tantor audio. Her short story, Break Time, and poetry has been featured in Mind's Eye literary magazine. The Kansas Writers Association published her short story, Existing Forces, appointing her as a noted author. She resides in Kansas with her husband, two children, and one-eyed beagle. As a member of the deaf and hard of hearing community, she incorporates sign language or deafness into every novel she writes.

https://www.authorstephaniehansen.com/

THANK YOU FOR READING

Did you enjoy this anthology?

We invite you to leave a review.

DID YOU KNOW THAT LEAVING A REVIEW…

Helps other readers find stories they might enjoy.
Gives you a chance to let your voice opinion.
Gives authors recognition for their hard work.
Doesn't have to be long.
A sentence or two about why you liked the book will do.